Magic Drum

&

Five More Amazing Short Stories

By

W. Salvage

Table of Contents

Goso, the Teacher

Once there was a man named
Go'so, who taught children to read,
not in a schoolhouse, but under a
calabash tree. One evening, while
Goso was sitting under the tree
deep in the study of the next day's
lessons, Paa, the gazelle, climbed
up the tree very quietly to steal
some fruit, and in so doing shook
off a calabash, which, in falling,
struck the teacher on the head and
killed him.

When his scholars came in the morning and found their teacher lying dead, they were filled with grief; so, after giving him a decent burial, they agreed among themselves to find the one who had killed Goso, and put him to death.

After talking the matter over they came to the conclusion that the south wind was the offender.

So they caught the south wind and beat it.

But the south wind cried: "Here! I am Koo'see, the south wind. Why are you beating me? What have I done?"

And they said: "Yes, we know you are Koosee; it was you who threw down the calabash that struck our teacher Goso. You should not have done it."

But Koosee said, "If I were so powerful would I be stopped by a mud wall?"

So they went to the mud wall and beat it.

But the mud wall cried: "Here! I am Keeyambaa'za, the mud wall. Why are you beating me? What have I done?"

And they said: "Yes, we know you are Keeyambaaza; it was you who stopped Koosee, the south wind; and Koosee, the south wind, threw down the calabash that struck our

teacher Goso. You should not have done it."

But Keeyambaaza said, "If I were so powerful would I be bored through by the rat?"

So they went and caught the rat and beat it.

But the rat cried: "Here! I am Paan'ya, the rat. Why are you beating me?
What have I done?"

And they said: "Yes, we know you are Paanya; it was you who bored through Keeyambaaza, the mud wall; which stopped Koosee, the south wind; and Koosee, the south wind, threw down the calabash that struck our teacher Goso. You should not have done it."

But Paanya said, "If I were so powerful would I be eaten by a cat?"

So they hunted for the cat, caught it, and beat it.

But the cat cried: "Here! I am Paa'ka, the cat. Why do you beat me?
What have I done?"

And they said: "Yes, we know you are Paaka; it is you that eats Paanya, the rat; who bores through Keeyambaaza, the mud wall; which stopped Koosee, the south wind; and Koosee, the south wind, threw down the calabash that struck our

teacher Goso. You should not have done it."

But Paaka said, "If I were so powerful would I be tied by a rope?"

So they took the rope and beat it.

But the rope cried: "Here! I am Kaam'ba, the rope. Why do you beat me? What have I done?"

And they said: "Yes, we know you are Kaamba; it is you that ties Paaka, the cat; who eats Paanya, the rat; who bores through Keeyambaaza, the mud wall; which stopped Koosee, the south wind; and Koosee, the south wind, threw down the calabash that struck our

teacher Goso. You should not have done it."

But Kaamba said, "If I were so powerful would I be cut by a knife?"

So they took the knife and beat it.

But the knife cried: "Here! I am Kee'soo, the knife. Why do you beat me? What have I done?"

And they said: "Yes, we know you are Keesoo; you cut Kaamba, the rope; that ties Paaka, the cat; who eats Paanya, the rat; who bores through Keeyambaaza, the mud wall; which stopped Koosee, the south wind; and
Koosee, the south wind, threw down the calabash that struck our teacher

Goso. You should not have done it."

But Keesoo said, "If I were so powerful would I be burned by the fire?"

And they went and beat the fire.

But the fire cried: "Here! I am Mo'to, the fire. Why do you beat me?
What have I done?"

And they said: "Yes, we know you are Moto; you burn Keesoo, the knife; that cuts Kaamba, the rope; that ties Paaka, the cat; who eats Paanya, the rat; who bores through Keeyambaaza, the mud wall; which stopped Koosee, the south wind; and Koosee, the south wind, threw down the calabash that struck our teacher Goso. You should not have done it."

But Moto said, "If I were so powerful would I be put out by water?"

And they went to the water and beat it.

But the water cried: "Here! I am Maa'jee, the water. Why do you beat me? What have I done?"

And they said: "Yes, we know you are Maajee; you put out Moto, the fire; that burns Keesoo, the knife; that cuts Kaamba, the rope; that ties Paaka, the cat; who eats Paanya, the rat; who bores through Keeyambaaza, the mud wall; which stopped Koosee, the south wind; and Koosee, the south wind, threw down the calabash that struck our teacher Goso. You should not have done it."

But Maajee said, "If I were so powerful would I be drunk by the ox?"

And they went to the ox and beat it.

But the ox cried: "Here! I am Ng'om'bay, the ox. Why do you beat me?
What have I done?"

And they said: "Yes, we know you are Ng'ombay; you drink Maajee, the water; that puts out Moto, the fire; that burns Keesoo, the knife; that cuts Kaamba, the rope; that ties Paaka, the cat; who eats Paanya, the rat; who bores through Keeyambaaza, the mud wall; which stopped Koosee, the south wind; and Koosee, the south wind, threw down the calabash that struck our teacher Goso. You should not have done it."

But Ng'ombay said, "If I were so powerful would I be tormented by the fly?"

And they caught a fly and beat it.

But the fly cried: "Here! I am Een'zee, the fly. Why do you beat me?
What have I done?"

And they said: "Yes, we know you are Eenzee; you torment

Ng'ombay, the ox; who drinks
Maajee, the water; that puts out
Moto, the fire; that burns Keesoo,
the knife; that cuts Kaamba, the
rope; that ties Paaka, the cat; who
eats Paanya, the rat; who bores
through Keeyambaaza, the mud
wall; which stopped Koosee, the
south wind; and Koosee, the south
wind, threw down the calabash that
struck our teacher Goso. You
should not have done it."

But Eenzee said, "If I were so
powerful would I be eaten by the
gazelle?"

And they searched for the gazelle,
and when they found it they beat it.

But the gazelle said: "Here! I am Paa, the gazelle. Why do you beat me?
What have I done?"

And they said: "Yes, we know you are Paa; you eat Eenzee, the fly; that torments Ng'ombay, the ox; who drinks Maajee, the water; that puts out Moto, the fire; that burns Keesoo, the knife; that cuts Kaamba, the rope; that ties Paaka, the cat; who eats Paanya, the rat; who bores through Keeyambaaza, the mud wall; which stopped Koosee, the south wind; and Koosee, the south wind, threw down the calabash that struck our teacher Goso. You should not have done it."

The gazelle, through surprise at being found out and fear of the consequences of his accidental killing of the teacher, while engaged in stealing, was struck dumb.

Then the scholars said: "Ah! he hasn't a word to say for himself. This is the fellow who threw down the calabash that struck our teacher Goso. We will kill him."

So they killed Paa, the gazelle, and avenged the death of their teacher.

Haamdaanee

Once there was a very poor man, named Haamdaa'nee, who begged from door to door for his living, sometimes taking things before they were offered him. After a while people became suspicious of him, and stopped giving him anything, in order to keep him away from their houses. So at last he was reduced to the necessity of going every morning to the village dust heap, and picking up and eating the few grains of the tiny little millet seed that he might find there.

One day, as he was scratching and turning over the heap, he found a dime, which he tied up in a corner of his ragged dress, and continued to hunt for millet grains, but could not find one.

"Oh, well," said he, "I've got a dime now; I'm pretty well fixed. I'll go home and take a nap instead of a meal."

So he went to his hut, took a drink of water, put some tobacco in his mouth, and went to sleep.

The next morning, as he scratched in the dust heap, he saw a countryman going along, carrying a basket made of twigs, and he called to him: "Hi, there, countryman! What have you in that cage?"

The countryman, whose name was Moohaad'eem, replied, "Gazelles."

And Haamdaanee called: "Bring them here. Let me see them."

Now there were three well-to-do men standing near; and when they saw the countryman coming to Haamdaanee they smiled, and said, "You're taking lots of trouble for nothing, Moohaadeem."

"How's that, gentlemen?" he inquired.

"Why," said they, "that poor fellow has nothing at all. Not a cent."

"Oh, I don't know that," said the countryman; "he may have plenty, for all I know."

"Not he," said they.

"Don't you see for yourself," continued one of them, "that he is on the dust heap? Every day he scratches there like a hen, trying to get enough grains of millet to keep himself alive. If he had any money, wouldn't he buy a square meal, for once in his life? Do you think he would want to buy a gazelle? What would he do with it? He can't find enough food for himself, without looking for any for a gazelle."

But Moohaadeem said: "Gentlemen, I have brought some goods here to sell. I answer all who call me, and if any one says 'Come,' I go to him. I don't favor one and slight another; therefore, as this man called me, I'm going to him."

"All right," said the first man; "you don't believe us. Well, we know where he lives, and all about him, and we know that he can't buy anything."

"That's so," said the second man. "Perhaps, however, you will see that we were right, after you have a talk with him."
To which the third man added, "Clouds are a sign of rain, but we have seen no signs of his being about to spend any money."

"All right, gentlemen," said Moohaadeem; "many better-looking people than he call me, and when I show them my gazelles they say, 'Oh, yes, they're very beautiful, but awfully dear; take them away.' So I shall not be disappointed if this man says the same thing. I shall go to him, anyhow."

Then one of the three men said, "Let us go with this man, and see what the beggar will buy."

"Pshaw!" said another; "buy! You talk foolishly. He has not had a good meal in three years, to my knowledge; and a man in his condition doesn't have money to buy gazelles. However, let's go; and if he makes this poor countryman carry his load over there just for the fun of looking at the gazelles, let each of us give him a good hard whack with our walkingsticks, to teach him how to behave toward honest merchants."

So, when they came near him, one of those three men said: "Well, here are the gazelles; now buy one. Here they are, you old hypocrite; you'll feast your eyes on them, but you can't buy them."

But Haamdaanee, paying no attention to the men, said to Moohaadeem,
"How much for one of your gazelles?"

Then another of those men broke in: "You're very innocent, aren't you? You know, as well as I do, that gazelles are sold every day at two for a quarter."

Still taking no notice of these outsiders, Haamdaanee continued, "I'd like to buy one for a dime."
"One for a dime!" laughed the men; "of course you'd like to buy

one for a dime. Perhaps you'd also like to have the dime to buy with."

Then one of them gave him a push on the cheek.

At this Haamdaanee turned and said: "Why do you push me on the cheek, when I've done nothing to you? I do not know you. I call this man, to transact some business with him, and you, who are strangers, step in to spoil our trade."

He then untied the knot in the corner of his ragged coat, produced the dime, and, handing it to Moohaadeem, said, "Please, good man, let me have a gazelle for that."

At this, the countryman took a small gazelle out of the cage and handed it to him, saying, "Here, master, take this one. I call it Keejee'paa." Then turning to those three men, he laughed, and said: "Ehe! How's this? You, with your white robes, and turbans, and swords, and daggers, and sandals on your feet—you gentlemen of property, and no mistake—you told me this man was too poor to buy anything; yet he has bought a gazelle for a dime, while you fine fellows, I think, haven't enough money among you to buy half a gazelle, if they were five cents each."

Then Moohaadeem and the three men went their several ways.

As for Haamdaanee, he stayed at the dust heap until he found a few grains of millet for himself and a few for Keejeepaa, the gazelle, and then went to his hut, spread his sleeping mat, and he and the gazelle slept together.
This going to the dust heap for a few grains of millet and then

going home to bed continued for about a week.

Then one night Haamdaanee was awakened by some one calling, "Master!" Sitting up, he answered: "Here I am. Who calls?" The gazelle answered, "I do!"

Upon this, the beggar man became so scared that he did not know whether he should faint or get up and run away.

Seeing him so overcome, Keejeepaa asked, "Why, master, what's the matter?"

"Oh, gracious!" he gasped; "what a wonder I see!"

"A wonder?" said the gazelle, looking all around; "why, what is this wonder, that makes you act as if you were all broken up?"

"Why, it's so wonderful, I can hardly believe I'm awake!" said his master. "Who in the world ever before knew of a gazelle that could speak?"

"Oho!" laughed Keejeepaa; "is that all? There are many more wonderful things than that. But now, listen, while I tell you why I called you."

"Certainly; I'll listen to every word," said the man. "I can't help listening!"

"Well, you see, it's just this way," said Keejeepaa; "I've allowed you to become my master, and I can not run away from you; so I want you to make an agreement with me, and I will make you a promise, and keep it."
"Say on," said his master.

"Now," continued the gazelle, "one doesn't have to be acquainted with you long, in order to discover that you are very poor. This scratching a few grains of millet from the dust heap every day, and managing to subsist upon them, is all very well for you—you're used to it, because it's a matter of necessity with you; but if I keep it up much longer, you won't have any gazelle—Keejeepaa will die of starvation. Therefore, I want to go away every day and feed on my own kind of food; and I promise you I will return every evening."

"Well, I guess I'll have to give my consent," said the man, in no very cheerful tone.

As it was now dawn, Keejeepaa jumped up and ran out of the door, Haamdaanee following him. The gazelle ran very fast, and his master stood watching him until he disappeared. Then tears started in the man's eyes, and, raising his hands, he cried, "Oh, my mother!" Then he cried, "Oh, my father!" Then he cried, "Oh, my gazelle! It has run away!"

Some of his neighbors, who heard him carrying on in this manner, took the opportunity to inform him that he was a fool, an idiot, and a dissipated fellow.

Said one of them: "You hung around that dust heap, goodness knows how long, scratching like a hen, till fortune gave you a dime. You hadn't sense enough to go and buy some decent food; you had to buy a gazelle. Now you've let the creature run away. What are you crying about? You brought all your trouble on yourself."

All this, of course, was very comforting to Haamdaanee, who slunk off to the dust heap, got a few grains of millet, and came back to his hut, which now seemed meaner and more desolate than ever.

At sunset, however, Keejeepaa came trotting in; and the beggar was happy again, and said, "Ah, my friend, you have returned to me."

"Of course," said the gazelle; "didn't I promise you? You see, I feel that when you bought me you gave all the money you had in the world, even though it was only a dime. Why, then, should I grieve you? I couldn't do it. If I go and get myself some food, I'll always come back evenings."

When the neighbors saw the gazelle come home every evening and run off every morning, they were greatly surprised, and began to suspect that Haamdaanee was a wizard.

Well, this coming and going continued for five days, the gazelle telling its master each night what fine places it had been to, and what lots of food it had eaten.

On the sixth day it was feeding among some thorn bushes in a thick wood, when, scratching away some bitter grass at the foot of a big tree, it saw an immense diamond of intense brightness.

"Oho!" said Keejeepaa, in great astonishment; "here's property, and no mistake! This is worth a kingdom! If I take it to my master he will be killed; for, being a poor man, if they say to him, 'Where did you get it?' and he answers, 'I picked it up,' they will not believe him; if he says, 'It was given to me,' they will not believe him either. It will not do for me to get my master into difficulties. I know what I'll do. I'll seek some powerful person; he will use it properly."

So Keejeepaa started off through the forest, holding the diamond in his mouth, and ran, and ran, but saw no town that day; so he slept in the forest, and arose at dawn and pursued his way. And the second day passed like the first.

On the third day the gazelle had traveled from dawn until between eight and nine o'clock, when he began to see scattered houses, getting larger in size, and knew he was approaching a town. In due time he found himself in the main street of a large city, leading direct to the sultan's palace, and began to run as fast as he could. People passing along stopped to look at the strange sight of a gazelle running swiftly along the main street with something wrapped in green leaves between its teeth.

The sultan was sitting at the door of his palace, when Keejeepaa, stopping a little way off, dropped the diamond from its mouth, and, lying down beside it, panting, called out: "Ho, there! Ho, there!" which is a cry every one makes in that part of the world when wishing to enter a house, remaining outside until the cry is answered.

After the cry had been repeated several times, the sultan said to his attendants, "Who is doing all that calling?"

And one answered, "Master, it's a gazelle that's calling, 'Ho, there!'"

"Ho-ho!" said the sultan; "Ho-ho! Invite the gazelle to come near."

Then three attendants ran to Keejeepaa and said: "Come, get up. The sultan commands you to come near."

So the gazelle arose, picked up the diamond, and, approaching the sultan, laid the jewel at his feet, saying, "Master, good afternoon!" To which the sultan replied: "May God make it good! Come near."

The sultan ordered his attendants to bring a carpet and a large cushion, and desired the gazelle to rest upon them. When it protested that it was comfortable as it was, he insisted, and Keejeepaa had to allow himself to be made a very honored guest. Then they brought milk and rice, and the sultan would hear nothing until the gazelle had fed and rested.

At last, when everything had been disposed of, the sultan said, "Well, now, my friend, tell me what news you bring."

And Keejeepaa said: "Master, I don't exactly know how you will like the news I bring. The fact is, I'm sent here to insult you! I've come to try and pick a quarrel with you! In fact, I'm here to propose a family alliance with you!"

At this the sultan exclaimed: "Oh, come! for a gazelle, you

certainly know how to talk! Now, the fact of it is, I'm looking for some one to insult me. I'm just aching to have some one pick a quarrel with me. I'm impatient for a family alliance. Go on with your message."

Then Keejeepaa said, "You don't bear any ill will against me, who am only a messenger?"

And the sultan said, "None at all."

"Well," said Keejeepaa, "look at this pledge I bring;" dropping the diamond wrapped in leaves into the sultan's lap.

When the sultan opened the leaves and saw the great, sparkling jewel, he was overcome with astonishment. At last he said, "Well?"

"I have brought this pledge," said the gazelle, "from my master, Sultan Daaraa'ee. He has heard that you have a daughter, so he sent you this jewel, hoping you will forgive him for not sending something more worthy of your acceptance than this trifle."

"Goodness!" said the sultan to himself; "he calls this a trifle!" Then to the gazelle: "Oh, that's all right; that's all right. I'm satisfied. The Sultan Daaraaee has my consent to marry my daughter, and I don't want a single thing from him. Let him come empty-handed. If he has more of these trifles, let him leave them at home. This is my message, and I hope you will make it perfectly clear to your master."

The gazelle assured him that he would explain everything satisfactorily, adding: "And now, master, I take my leave. I go straight to our own town, and hope that in about eleven days we shall return to be your guests." So, with mutual compliments, they parted.

In the meantime, Haamdaanee was having an exceedingly tough time. Keejeepaa having disappeared, he wandered about the town moaning, "Oh, my poor gazelle! my poor gazelle!" while the neighbors laughed and jeered at him, until, between them and his loss, he was nearly out of his mind.

But one evening, when he had gone to bed, Keejeepaa walked in. Up he jumped, and began to embrace the gazelle, and weep over it, and carry on at a great rate.

When he thought there had been about enough of this kind of thing, the gazelle said: "Come, come; keep quiet, my master. I've brought you good news." But the beggar man continued to cry and fondle, and declare that he had thought his gazelle was dead.

At last Keejeepaa said: "Oh, well, master, you see I'm all right. You must brace up, and prepare to hear my news, and do as I advise you."

"Go on; go on," replied his master; "explain what you will, I'll do whatever you require me to do. If you were to say, 'Lie down on your back, that I may roll you over the side of the hill,' I would lie down."

"Well," said the gazelle, "there is not much to explain just now, but I'll tell you this: I've seen many kinds of food, food that is desirable and food that is objectionable, but this food I'm about to offer you is very sweet indeed."

"What?" said Haamdaanee. "Is it possible that in this world

there is anything that is positively good? There must be good and bad in everything. Food that is both sweet and bitter is good food, but if food were nothing but sweetness would it not be injurious?"

"H'm!" yawned the gazelle; "I'm too tired to talk philosophy. Let's go to sleep now, and when I call you in the morning, all you have to do is to get up and follow me."

So at dawn they set forth, the gazelle leading the way, and for five days they journeyed through the forest.

On the fifth day they came to a stream, and Keejeepaa said to his master, "Lie down here." When he had done so, the gazelle set to and beat him so soundly that he cried out: "Oh, let up, I beg of you!"

"Now," said the gazelle, "I'm going away, and when I return I expect to find you right here; so don't you leave this spot on any account." Then he ran away, and about ten o'clock that morning he arrived at the house of the sultan.

Now, ever since the day Keejeepaa left the town, soldiers had been placed along the road to watch for and announce the approach of Sultan Daaraaee; so one of them, when he saw the gazelle in the distance, rushed up and cried to the sultan, "Sultan Daaraaee is coming! I've seen the gazelle running as fast as it can in this direction."

The sultan and his attendants immediately set out to meet his guests; but when they had gone a little way beyond the town they met the gazelle coming along alone, who, on reaching the sultan, said, "Good day, my master." The sultan replied in kind, and asked the news, but

Keejeepaa said: "Ah, do not ask me. I can scarcely walk, and my news is bad!"

"Why, how is that?" asked the sultan.

"Oh, dear!" sighed the gazelle; "such misfortune and misery! You see, Sultan Daaraaee and I started alone to come here, and we got along all right until we came to the thick part of the forest yonder, when we were met by robbers, who seized my master, bound him, beat him, and took everything he had, even stripping off every stitch of his clothing. Oh, dear! oh, dear!"

"Dear me!" said the sultan; "we must attend to this at once." So, hurrying back with his attendants to his house, he called a groom, to whom he said, "Saddle the best horse in my stable, and put on him my finest harness." Then he directed a woman servant to open the big inlaid chest and bring him a bag of clothes. When she brought it he picked out a loin-cloth, and a long white robe, and a black overjacket, and a shawl for the waist, and a turban cloth, all of the very finest. Then he sent for a curved sword with a gold hilt, and a curved dagger with gold filigree, and a pair of elegant sandals, and a fine walking-cane.

Then the sultan said to Keejeepaa, "Take some of my soldiers, and let them convey these things to Sultan Daaraaee, that he may dress himself and come to me."

But the gazelle answered: "Ah, my master, can I take these soldiers with me and put Sultan Daaraaee to shame? There he lies, beaten and robbed, and I would not have any one see him. I can take everything by myself."

"Why," exclaimed the sultan, "here is a horse, and there are clothes and arms. I don't see how a little gazelle can manage all those things."

But the gazelle had them fasten everything on the horse's back, and tie the end of the bridle around his own neck, and then he set off alone, amidst the wonder and admiration of the people of that city, high and low.

When he arrived at the place where he had left the beggar-man, he found him lying waiting for him, and overjoyed at his return.

"Now," said he, "I have brought you the sweet food I promised. Come, get up and bathe yourself."

With the hesitation of a person long unaccustomed to such a thing, the man stepped into the stream and began to wet himself a little.

"Oh," said the gazelle, impatiently, "a little water like that won't do you much good; get out into the deep pool."

"Dear me!" said the man, timidly; "there is so much water there; and where there is much water there are sure to be horrible animals."

"Animals! What kind of animals?"

"Well, crocodiles, water lizards, snakes, and, at any rate, frogs; and they bite people, and I'm terribly afraid of all of them."

"Oh, well," said Keejeepaa, "do the best you can in the stream; but rub yourself well with earth, and, for goodness' sake, scrub your teeth well with sand; they are awfully dirty."

So the man obeyed, and soon made quite a change in his appearance.

Then the gazelle said: "Here, hurry up and put on these things. The sun has gone down, and we ought to have started before this."

So the man dressed himself in the fine clothes the sultan had sent, and then he mounted the horse, and they started; the gazelle trotting on ahead.

When they had gone some distance, the gazelle stopped, and said, "See here: nobody who sees you now would suspect that you are the man who scratched in the dust heap yesterday. Even if we were to go back to our town the neighbors would not recognize you, if it were only for the fact that your face is clean and your teeth are white. Your appearance is all right, but I have a caution to give you. Over there, where we are going, I have procured for you the sultan's daughter for a wife, with all the usual wedding gifts. Now, you must keep quiet. Say nothing except, 'How d'ye do?' and 'What's the news?' Let me do the talking."

"All right," said the man; "that suits me exactly."

"Do you know what your name is?"

"Of course I do."

"Indeed? Well, what is it?"

"Why, my name is Haamdaanee."

"Not much," laughed Keejeepaa; "your name is Sultan Daaraaee."

"Oh, is it?" said his master. "That's good."

So they started forward again, and in a little while they saw soldiers running in every direction, and fourteen of these joined them to escort them. Then they saw ahead of them the sultan, and the vizirs, and the emirs, and the judges, and the great men of the city, coming to meet them.

"Now, then," said Keejeepaa, "get off your horse and salute your fatherin-law. That's him in the middle, wearing the sky-blue jacket."

"All right," said the man, jumping off his horse, which was then led by a soldier.

So the two met, and the sultans shook hands, and kissed each other, and walked up to the palace together.

Then they had a great feast, and made merry and talked until night, at which time Sultan Daaraaee and the gazelle were put into an inner room, with three soldiers at the door to guard and attend upon them.

When the morning came, Keejeepaa went to the sultan and said: "Master, we wish to attend to the business which brought us here. We want to marry your daughter, and the sooner the ceremony takes place, the better it will please the Sultan Daaraaee."

"Why, that's all right," said the sultan; "the bride is ready. Let some one call the teacher, Mwaalee'moo, and tell him to come at once."

When Mwaaleemoo arrived, the sultan said, "See here, we want you to marry this gentleman to my daughter right away."

"All right; I'm ready," said the teacher. So they were married.

Early the next morning the gazelle said to his master: "Now I'm off on a journey. I shall be gone about a week; but however long I am gone, don't you leave the house till I return. Good-bye."

Then he went to the real sultan and said: "Good master, Sultan

Daaraaee has ordered me to return to our town and put his house in order; he commands me to be here again in a week; if I do not return by that time, he will stay here until I come."

The sultan asked him if he would not like to have some soldiers go with him; but the gazelle replied that he was quite competent to take care of himself, as his previous journeys had proved, and he preferred to go alone; so with mutual good wishes they parted.

But Keejeepaa did not go in the direction of the old village. He struck off by another road through the forest, and after a time came to a very fine town, of large, handsome houses. As he went through the principal street, right to the far end, he was greatly astonished to observe that the town seemed to have no inhabitants, for he saw neither man, woman, nor child in all the place.

At the end of the main street he came upon the largest and most beautiful house he had ever seen, built of sapphire, and turquoise, and costly marbles.

"Oh, my!" said the gazelle; "this house would just suit my master. I'll have to pluck up my courage and see whether this is deserted like the other houses in this mysterious town."

So Keejeepaa knocked at the door, and called, "Hullo, there!" several times; but no one answered. And he said to himself: "This is strange! If there were no one inside, the door would be fastened on the outside. Perhaps they are in another part of the house, or asleep. I'll call again, louder."

So he called again, very loud and long, "Hul-lo, th-e-re! Hul-lo!" And directly an old woman inside answered, "Who is that calling so loudly?"

"It is I, your grandchild, good mistress," said Keejeepaa.

"If you are my grandchild," replied the old woman, "go back to your home at once; don't come and die here, and bring me to my death also."

"Oh, come," said he, "open the door, mistress; I have just a few words I wish to say to you."

"My dear grandson," she replied, "the only reason why I do not open the door is because I fear to endanger both your life and my own."

"Oh, don't worry about that; I guess your life and mine are safe enough for a while. Open the door, anyhow, and hear the little I have to say."

So the old woman opened the door.

Then they exchanged salutations and compliments, after which she asked the gazelle, "What's the news from your place, grandson?"

"Oh, everything is going along pretty well," said he; "what's the news around here?"

"Ah!" sighed the old creature; "the news here is very bad. If you're looking for a place to die in, you've struck it here. I've not the slightest doubt you'll see all you want of death this very day."

"Huh!" replied Keejeepaa, lightly; "for a fly to die in honey is not bad for the fly, and doesn't injure the honey."

"It may be all very well for you to be easy about it," persisted the old person; "but if people with swords and shields did not escape, how can a little thing like you avoid danger? I must again beg of you to go back to the place you came from. Your safety seems of more interest to me than it is to you."

"Well, you see, I can't go back just now; and besides, I want to find out more about this place. Who owns it?"

"Ah, grandson, in this house are enormous wealth, numbers of people, hundreds of horses, and the owner is Neeo'ka Mkoo', the wonderfully big snake. He owns this whole town, also."

"Oho! Is that so?" said Keejeepaa. "Look here, old lady; can't you put me on to some plan of getting near this big snake, that I may kill him?"

"Mercy!" cried the old woman, in affright; "don't talk like that. You've put my life in danger already, for I'm sure Neeoka Mkoo can hear what is said in this house, wherever he is. You see I'm a poor old woman, and I have been placed here, with those pots and pans, to cook for him. Well, when the big snake is coming, the wind begins to blow and the dust flies as it would do in a great storm. Then, when he arrives in the courtyard, he eats until he is full, and after that, goes inside there to drink water. When he has finished, he goes away again. This occurs every other day, just when the sun is overhead. I may add that Neeoka Mkoo has seven heads. Now, then, do you think yourself a match for him?"

"Look here, mother," said the gazelle, "don't you worry about me. Has this big snake a sword?"

"He has. This is it," said she, taking from its peg a very keen and beautiful blade, and handing it to him; "but what's the use in bothering about it? We are dead already."

"We shall see about that," said Keejeepaa.

Just at that moment the wind began to blow, and the dust to fly, as if a great storm were approaching.

"Do you hear the great one coming?" cried the old woman.

"Pshaw!" said the gazelle; "I'm a great one also—and I have the advantage of being on the inside. Two bulls can't live in one cattle-pen.
Either he will live in this house, or I will."

Notwithstanding the terror the old lady was in, she had to smile at the assurance of this little undersized gazelle, and repeated over again her account of the people with swords and shields who had been killed by the big snake.

"Ah, stop your gabbling!" said the gazelle; "you can't always judge a banana by its color or size. Wait and see, grandma."

In a very little while the big snake, Neeoka Mkoo, came into the courtyard, and went around to all the pots and ate their contents. Then he came to the door.

"Hullo, old lady," said he; "how is it I smell a new kind of odor inside there?"

"Oh, that's nothing, good master," replied the old woman; "I've been so busy around here lately I haven't had time to look after myself; but this morning I used some perfume, and that's what you smell."

Now, Keejeepaa had drawn the sword, and was standing just inside the doorway; so, when the big snake put his head in, it was cut off so quickly that its owner did not know it was gone. When he put in his second head it was cut off with the same quickness; and, feeling a little irritation, he exclaimed, "Who's inside there, scratching me?" He then thrust in his third head, and that was cut off also.

This continued until six heads had been disposed of, when

Neeoka Mkoo unfolded his rings and lashed around so that the gazelle and the old woman could not see one another through the dust.

Then the snake thrust in his seventh head, and the gazelle, crying: "Now your time has come; you've climbed many trees, but this you can not climb," severed it, and immediately fell down in a fainting fit.

Well, that old woman, although she was seventy-five years of age, jumped, and shouted, and laughed, like a girl of nine. Then she ran and got water, and sprinkled the gazelle, and turned him this way and that way, until at last he sneezed; which greatly pleased the old person, who fanned him and tended him until he was quite recovered.

"Oh, my!" said she; "who would have thought you could be a match for him, my grandson?"

"Well, well," said Keejeepaa; "that's all over. Now show me everything around this place."

So she showed him everything, from top to bottom: store-rooms full of goods, chambers full of expensive foods, rooms containing handsome people who had been kept prisoners for a long time, slaves, and everything.

Next he asked her if there was any person who was likely to lay claim to the place or make any trouble; and she answered: "No one; everything here belongs to you."

"Very well, then," said he, "you stay here and take care of these things until I bring my master. This place belongs to him now."

Keejeepaa stayed three days examining the house, and said to himself: "Well, when my master comes here he will be much pleased with what I have done for him, and he'll appreciate it after the life he's been accustomed to. As to his father-in-law, there is not a house in his town that can compare with this."

On the fourth day he departed, and in due time arrived at the town where the sultan and his master lived. Then there were great rejoicings; the sultan being particularly pleased at his return, while his master felt as if he had received a new lease of life.

After everything had settled down a little, Keejeepaa told his master he must be ready to go, with his wife, to his new home after four days. Then he went and told the sultan that Sultan Daaraaee desired to take his wife to his own town in four days; to which the sultan strongly objected; but the gazelle said it was his master's wish, and at last everything was arranged.

On the day of the departure a great company assembled to

escort Sultan Daaraaee and his bride. There were the bride's ladies-in-waiting, and slaves, and horsemen, and Keejeepaa leading them all.

So they traveled three days, resting when the sun was overhead, and stopping each evening about five o'clock to eat and sleep; arising next morning at day-break, eating, and going forward again. And all this time the gazelle took very little rest, going all through the company, from the ladies to the slaves, and seeing that every one was well supplied with food and quite comfortable; therefore the entire company loved him and valued him like the apples of their eyes.

On the fourth day, during the afternoon, many houses came into view, and some of the folks called Keejeepaa's attention to them. "Certainly," said he; "that is our town, and that house you see yonder is the palace of Sultan Daaraaee."

So they went on, and all the company filed into the courtyard, while the gazelle and his master went into the house.

When the old woman saw Keejeepaa, she began to dance, and shout, and carry on, just as she did when he killed Neeoka Mkoo, and taking up his foot she kissed it; but Keejeepaa said: "Old lady, let me alone; the one to be made much of is this my master, Sultan Daaraaee. Kiss his feet; he has the first honors whenever he is present."

The old woman excused herself for not knowing the master, and then Sultan Daaraaee and the gazelle went around on a tour of inspection. The sultan ordered all the prisoners to be released, the horses to be sent out to pasture, all the rooms to be swept, the furniture to be dusted, and, in the meantime, servants were busy preparing food. Then every one had apartments assigned to him, and all were satisfied.

After they had remained there some time, the ladies who had accompanied the bride expressed a desire to return to their own homes. Keejeepaa begged them not to hurry away, but after a while they departed, each loaded with gifts by the gazelle, for whom they had a thousand times more affection than for his master. Then things settled down to their regular routine.

One day the gazelle said to the old woman: "I think the conduct of my master is very singular. I have done nothing but good for him all the time I have been with him. I came to this town and braved many dangers for him, and when all was over I gave everything to him. Yet he has never asked: 'How did you get this house? How did you get this town? Who is the owner of this house? Have you rented all these things, or have they been given you? What has become of the inhabitants of the place?' I don't understand him. And further: although I have done nothing but good for him, he has never done one good thing for me. Nothing here is really his. He never saw such a house or town as this since the day he was born, and he doesn't own anything of it. I believe the old folks were right when they said, 'If you want to do any person good, don't do too much; do him a little harm occasionally, and he'll think more of you.' However, I've done all I can now, and I'd like to see him make some little return."

Next morning the old woman was awakened early by the gazelle calling, "Mother! Mother!" When she went to him she found he was sick in his stomach, feverish, and all his legs ached.

"Go," said he, "and tell my master I am very ill."

So she went upstairs and found the master and mistress sitting on a marble couch, covered with a striped silk scarf from India.

"Well," said the master, "what do you want, old woman?"

"Oh, my master," cried she, "Keejeepaa is sick!"

The mistress started and said: "Dear me! What is the matter with him?"

"All his body pains him. He is sick all over."

"Oh, well," said the master, "what can I do? Go and get some of that red millet, that is too common for our use, and make him some gruel."

"Gracious!" exclaimed his wife, staring at him in amazement;

"do you wish her to feed our friend with stuff that a horse would not eat if he were ever so hungry? This is not right of you." "Ah, get out!" said he, "you're crazy. We eat rice; isn't red millet good enough for a gazelle that cost only a dime?"

"Oh, but he is no ordinary gazelle. He should be as dear to you as the apple of your eye. If sand got in your eye it would trouble you."

"You talk too much," returned her husband; then, turning to the old woman, he said, "Go and do as I told you."

So the old woman went downstairs, and when she saw the gazelle, she began to cry, and say, "Oh, dear! oh, dear!"

It was a long while before the gazelle could persuade her to tell him what had passed upstairs, but at last she told him all. When he had heard it, he said: "Did he really tell you to make me red millet gruel?"

"Ah," cried she, "do you think I would say such a thing if it were not so?"

"Well," said Keejeepaa, "I believe what the old folks said was right. However, we'll give him another chance. Go up to him again, and tell him I am very sick, and that I can't eat that gruel."

So she went upstairs, and found the master and mistress sitting by the window, drinking coffee.

The master, looking around and seeing her, said: "What's the matter now, old woman?"

And she said: "Master, I am sent by Keejeepaa. He is very sick indeed, and has not taken the gruel you told me to make for him."

"Oh, bother!" he exclaimed. "Hold your tongue, and keep your feet still, and shut your eyes, and stop your ears with wax; then, if that gazelle tells you to come up here, say that your legs are stiff; and if he tells you to listen, say your ears are deaf; and if he tells you to look, say your sight has failed you; and if he wants you to talk, tell him your tongue is paralyzed."

When the old woman heard these words, she stood and stared, and was unable to move. As for his wife, her face became sad, and the tears began to start from her eyes; observing which, her husband said, sharply, "What's the matter with you, sultan's daughter?"

The lady replied, "A man's madness is his undoing."

"Why do you say that, mistress?" he inquired.

"Ah," said she, "I am grieved, my husband, at your treatment of Keejeepaa. Whenever I say a good word for the gazelle you dislike to hear it. I pity you that your understanding is gone."

"What do you mean by talking in that manner to me?" he blustered.

"Why, advice is a blessing, if properly taken. A husband should advise with his wife, and a wife with her husband; then they are both blessed."

"Oh, stop," said her husband, impatiently; "it's evident you've lost your senses. You should be chained up." Then he said to the old woman: "Never mind her talk; and as to this gazelle, tell him to stop bothering me and putting on style, as if he were the sultan. I can't eat, I can't drink, I can't sleep, because of that gazelle worrying me with his messages. First, the gazelle is sick; then, the gazelle doesn't like what he gets to eat. Confound it! If he likes to eat, let him eat; if he doesn't like to eat, let him die and be out of the way. My mother is dead, and my father is dead, and I still live and eat; shall I be put out of my way by a gazelle, that I bought for a dime, telling me he wants this thing or that thing? Go and tell him to learn how to behave himself toward his superiors."

When the old woman went downstairs, she found the gazelle was bleeding at the mouth, and in a very bad way. All she could say was, "My son, the good you did is all lost; but be patient."

And the gazelle wept with the old woman when she told him all that had passed, and he said, "Mother, I am dying, not only from sickness, but from shame and anger at this man's ingratitude."

After a while Keejeepaa told the old woman to go and tell the master that he believed he was dying. When she went upstairs she found Daaraaee chewing sugar-cane, and she said to him, "Master, the gazelle is worse; we think him nearer to dying than getting well."

To which he answered: "Haven't I told you often enough not to bother me?"

Then his wife said: "Oh, husband, won't you go down and see the poor gazelle? If you don't like to go, let me go and see him. He never gets a single good thing from you."

But he turned to the old woman and said, "Go and tell that nuisance of a gazelle to die eleven times if he chooses to."

"Now, husband," persisted the lady, "what has Keejeepaa done to you?
Has he done you any wrong? Such words as yours people use to their enemies only. Surely the gazelle is not your enemy. All the people who know him, great and lowly, love him dearly, and they will think it very wrong of you if you neglect him. Now, do be kind to him, Sultan Daaraaee."

But he only repeated his assertion that she had lost her wits, and would have nothing further of argument.

So the old woman went down and found the gazelle worse than ever.

In the meantime Sultan Daaraaee's wife managed to give some rice to a servant to cook for the gazelle, and also sent him a soft shawl to cover him and a pillow to lie upon. She also sent him a message that if he wished, she would have her father's best physicians attend him.

All this was too late, however, for just as these good things arrived, Keejeepaa died.

When the people heard he was dead, they went running around crying and having an awful time; and when Sultan Daaraaee found out what all the commotion was about he was very indignant, remarking, "Why, you are making as much fuss as if I were dead, and all over a gazelle that I bought for a dime!"

But his wife said: "Husband, it was this gazelle that came to ask me of my father, it was he who brought me from my father's, and it was to him I was given by my father. He gave you everything good, and you do not possess a thing that he did not procure for you. He did everything he could to help you, and you not only returned him unkindness, but now he is dead you have ordered people to throw him into the well. Let us alone, that we may weep."

But the gazelle was taken and thrown into the well.

Then the lady wrote a letter telling her father to come to her directly, and despatched it by trusty messengers; upon the receipt of which the sultan and his attendants started hurriedly to visit his daughter.

When they arrived, and heard that the gazelle was dead and had been thrown into the well, they wept very much; and the sultan, and the vizir, and the judges, and the rich chief men, all went down into the well and brought up the body of Keejeepaa, and took it away with them and buried it.

Now, that night the lady dreamt that she was at home at her father's house; and when dawn came she awoke and found she was in her own bed in her own town again.

And her husband dreamed that he was on the dust heap, scratching; and when he awoke there he was, with both hands full of dust, looking for grains of millet. Staring wildly he looked around to the right and left, saying: "Oh, who has played this trick on me? How did I get back here, I wonder?"

Just then the children going along, and seeing him, laughed and hooted at him, calling out: "Hullo, Haamdaanee, where have you been? Where do you come from? We thought you were dead long ago."

So the sultan's daughter lived in happiness with her people until the end, and that beggar-man continued to scratch for grains of millet in the dust heap until he died.

If this story is good, the goodness belongs to all; if it is bad, the badness belongs only to him who told it.

The King's Magic Drum

Efriam Duke was an ancient king of Calabar. He was a peaceful man, and did not like war. He had a wonderful drum, the property of which, when it was beaten, was always to provide plenty of good food and drink. So whenever any country declared war against him, he used to call all his enemies together and beat his drum;

then to the surprise of every one, instead of fighting the people found tables spread with all sorts of dishes, fish, foo-foo, palm-oil chop, soup, cooked yams and ocros, and plenty of palm wine for everybody. In this way he kept all the country quiet, and sent his enemies away with full stomachs, and in a happy and contented frame of mind. There was only one drawback to possessing the drum, and that was, if the owner of the drum walked over any stick on the road or stept over a fallen tree, all the food would immediately go bad, and three hundred Egbo men would appear with sticks and whips and beat the owner of the drum and all the invited guests very severely.

Efriam Duke was a rich man. He had many farms and hundreds of slaves, a large store of kernels on the beach, and many puncheons of palmoil. He also had fifty wives and many children. The wives were all fine women and healthy; they were also good mothers, and all of them had plenty of children, which was good for the king's house.

Every few months the king used to issue invitations to all his subjects to come to a big feast, even the wild animals were invited; the elephants, hippopotami, leopards, bush cows, and antelopes used to come, for in those days there was no trouble, as they were friendly with man, and when they were at the feast they did not kill one another. All the people and the animals as well were envious of the king's drum and wanted to possess it, but the king would not part with it.

One morning Ikwor Edem, one of the king's wives, took her little daughter down to the spring to wash her, as she was covered with yaws, which are bad sores all over the body. The tortoise happened to be up a palm tree, just over the spring, cutting nuts for his midday meal; and while he was cutting, one of the nuts fell to the ground, just in front of the child. The little girl, seeing the good food, cried for it, and the mother, not knowing any better, picked up the palm nut and gave it to her daughter. Directly the tortoise saw this he climbed down the tree, and asked the woman where his palm nut was. She replied that she had given it to her child to eat. Then the tortoise, who very much wanted the king's drum, thought he would make plenty palaver over this and force the king to give him the drum, so he said to the mother of the child—

"I am a poor man, and I climbed the tree to get food for myself and my family. Then you took my palm nut and gave it to your child. I shall tell the whole matter to the king, and see what he has to say when he hears that one of his wives has stolen my food," for this, as every one knows, is a very serious crime according to native custom.

Ikwor Edem then said to the tortoise—

"I saw your palm nut lying on the ground, and thinking it had fallen from the tree, I gave it to my little girl to eat, but I did not steal it. My husband the king is a rich man, and if you have any complaint to make against me or my child, I will take you before him."

So when she had finished washing her daughter at the spring she took the tortoise to her husband, and told him what had taken place. The king then asked the tortoise what he would accept as compensation for the loss of his palm nut, and offered him money, cloth, kernels or palm-oil, all of which things the tortoise refused one after the other.

The king then said to the tortoise, "What will you take? You may have anything you like."

And the tortoise immediately pointed to the king's drum, and said that it was the only thing he wanted.

In order to get rid of the tortoise the king said, "Very well, take the drum," but he never told the tortoise about the bad things that would happen to him if he stept over a fallen tree, or walked over a stick on the road.

The tortoise was very glad at this, and carried the drum home in triumph to his wife, and said, "I am now a rich man, and shall do no more work. Whenever I want food, all I have to do is to beat this drum, and food will immediately be brought to me, and plenty to drink."

His wife and children were very pleased when they heard this, and asked the tortoise to get food at once, as they were all hungry. This the tortoise was only too pleased to do, as he wished to show off his newly acquired wealth, and was also rather hungry himself, so he beat the drum in the same way as he had seen the king do when he wanted something to eat, and immediately plenty of food appeared, so they all sat down and made a great feast. The tortoise did this for three days, and everything went well; all his children got fat, and had as much as they could possibly eat. He was therefore very proud of his drum, and in order to display his riches he sent invitations to the king and all the people and animals to come to a feast. When the people received their invitations they laughed, as they knew the tortoise was very poor, so very few attended the feast; but the king, knowing about the drum, came, and when the tortoise beat the drum, the food was brought as usual in great profusion, and all the people sat down and enjoyed their meal very much. They were much astonished that the poor tortoise should be able to entertain so many people, and told all their friends what fine dishes had been placed before them, and that they had never had a better dinner. The people who had not gone were very sorry when they heard this, as a good feast, at somebody else's expense, is not provided every day. After the feast all the people looked upon the tortoise as one of the richest men in the kingdom, and he was very much respected in consequence. No one, except the king, could understand how the poor tortoise could suddenly entertain so lavishly, but they all made up their minds that if the tortoise ever gave another feast, they would not refuse again.

When the tortoise had been in possession of the drum for a few weeks he became lazy and did no work, but went about the country boasting of his riches, and took to drinking too much. One day after he had been drinking a lot of palm wine at a distant farm, he started home carrying his drum; but having had too much to drink, he did not notice a stick in the path. He walked over the stick, and of course the Ju Ju was broken at once. But he did not know this, as nothing happened at the time, and eventually he arrived at his house very tired, and still not very well from having drunk too much. He threw the drum into a corner and went to sleep. When he woke up in the morning the tortoise began to feel hungry, and as his wife and children were calling out for food, he beat the drum; but instead of food being brought, the house was filled with Egbo men, who beat the tortoise, his wife and children, badly. At this the tortoise was very angry, and said to himself—

"I asked every one to a feast, but only a few came, and they had plenty to eat and drink. Now, when I want food for myself and my family, the Egbos come and beat me. Well, I will let the other people share the same fate, as I do not see why I and my family should be beaten when I have given a feast to all people."

He therefore at once sent out invitations to all the men and animals to come to a big dinner the next day at three o'clock in the afternoon.

When the time arrived many people came, as they did not wish to lose the chance of a free meal a second time. Even the sick men, the lame, and the blind got their friends to lead them to the feast. When they had all arrived, with the exception of the king and his wives, who sent excuses, the tortoise beat his drum as usual, and then quickly hid himself under a bench, where he could not be seen. His wife and children he had sent away before the feast, as he knew what would surely happen. Directly he had beaten the drum three hundred Egbo men appeared with whips, and started flogging all the guests, who could not escape, as the doors had been fastened. The beating went on for two hours, and the people were so badly punished, that many of them had to be carried home on the backs of their friends. The leopard was the only one who escaped, as directly he saw the Egbo men arrive he knew that things were likely to be unpleasant, so he gave a big spring and jumped right out of the compound.

When the tortoise was satisfied with the beating the people had received he crept to the door and opened it. The people then ran away, and when the tortoise gave a certain tap on the drum all the Egbo men vanished. The people who had been beaten were so angry, and made so much palaver with the tortoise, that he made up his mind to return the drum to the king the next day. So in the morning the tortoise went to the king and brought the drum with him. He told the king that he was not satisfied with the drum, and wished to exchange it for something else; he did not mind so much what the king gave him so long as he got full value for the drum, and he was quite willing to accept a certain number of slaves, or a few farms, or their equivalent in cloth or rods.

The king, however, refused to do this; but as he was rather sorry for the tortoise, he said he would present him with a magic foo-foo tree, which would provide the tortoise and his family with food, provided he kept a certain condition. This the tortoise gladly consented to do. Now this foo-foo tree only bore fruit once a year, but every day it dropped foo-foo and soup on the ground. And the condition was, that the owner should gather sufficient food for the day, once, and not return again for more. The tortoise, when he had thanked the king for his generosity, went home to his wife and told her to bring her calabashes to the tree. She did so, and they gathered plenty of foo-foo and soup quite sufficient for the whole family for that day, and went back to their house very happy.

That night they all feasted and enjoyed themselves. But one of the sons, who was very greedy, thought to himself—

"I wonder where my father gets all this good food from? I must ask him."

So in the morning he said to his father—

"Tell me where do you get all this foo-foo and soup from?"

But his father refused to tell him, as his wife, who was a cunning woman, said—

"If we let our children know the secret of the foo-foo tree, some day when they are hungry, after we have got our daily supply, one of them may go to the tree and gather more, which will break the Ju Ju."

But the envious son, being determined to get plenty of food for himself, decided to track his father to the place where he obtained the food. This was rather difficult to do, as the tortoise always went out alone, and took the greatest care to prevent any one following him. The boy, however, soon thought of a plan, and got a calabash with a long neck and a hole in the end. He filled the calabash with wood ashes, which he obtained from the fire, and then got a bag which his father always carried on his back when he went out to get food. In the bottom of the bag the boy then made a small hole, and inserted the calabash with the neck downwards, so that when his father walked to the foo-foo tree he would leave a small trail of wood ashes behind him. Then when his father, having slung his bag over his back as usual, set out to get the daily supply of food, his greedy son followed the trail of the wood ashes, taking great care to hide himself and not to let his father perceive that he was being followed. At last the tortoise arrived at the tree, and placed his calabashes on the ground and collected the food for the day, the boy watching him from a distance. When his father had finished and went home the boy also returned, and having had a good meal, said nothing to his parents, but went to bed. The next morning he got some of his brothers, and after his father had finished getting the daily supply, they went to the tree and collected much foo-foo and soup, and so broke the Ju Ju.

At daylight the tortoise went to the tree as usual, but he could not find it, as during the night the whole bush had grown up, and the foo-foo tree was hidden from sight. There was nothing to be seen but a dense mass of prickly tie-tie palm. Then the tortoise at once knew that some one had broken the Ju Ju, and had gathered foo-foo from the tree twice in the same day; so he returned very sadly to his house, and told his wife. He then called all his family together and told them what had happened, and asked them who had done this evil thing. They all denied having had anything to do with the tree, so the tortoise in despair brought all his family to the place where the foo-foo tree had been, but which was now all prickly tie-tie palm, and said

—

"My dear wife and children, I have done all that I can for you, but you have broken my Ju Ju; you must therefore for the future live on the tie-tie palm."

So they made their home underneath the prickly tree, and from that day you will always find tortoises living under the prickly tie-tie palm, as they have nowhere else to go to for food.

The Story of the Drummer and the Alligators

There was once a woman named Affiong Any who lived at 'Nsidung, a small town to the south of Calabar. She was married to a chief of Hensham Town called Etim Ekeng. They had lived together for several years, but had no children. The chief was very anxious to have a child during his lifetime, and made sacrifices to his Ju Ju, but they had no effect. So he went to a witch man, who told him that the reason he had no children was that he was too rich. The chief then asked the witch man how he should spend his money in order to get a child, and he was told to make friends with everybody, and give big feasts, so that he should get rid of some of his money and become poorer.

The chief then went home and told his wife. The next day his wife called all her company together and gave them a big dinner, which cost a lot of money; much food was consumed, and large quantities of tombo were drunk. Then the chief entertained his company, which cost a lot more money. He also wasted a lot of money in the Egbo house. When half of his property was wasted, his wife told him that she had conceived. The chief, being very glad, called a big play for the next day.

In those days all the rich chiefs of the country belonged to the Alligator Company, and used to meet in the water. The reason they belonged to the company was, first of all, to protect their canoes when they went trading, and secondly, to destroy the canoes and property of the people who did not belong to their company, and to take their money and kill their slaves.

Chief Etim Ekeng was a kind man, and would not join this society, although he was repeatedly urged to do so. After a time a son was born to the chief, and he called him Edet Etim. The chief then called the Egbo society together, and all the doors of the houses in the town were shut, the markets were stopped, and the women were not allowed to go outside their houses while the Egbo was playing. This was kept up for several days, and cost the chief a lot of money. Then he made up his mind that he would divide his property, and give his son half when he became old enough. Unfortunately after three months the chief died, leaving his sorrowing wife to look after their little child.

The wife then went into mourning for seven years for her husband, and after that time she became entitled to all his property, as the late chief had no brothers. She looked after the little boy very carefully until he grew up, when he became a very fine, healthy young man, and was much admired by all the pretty girls of the town; but his mother warned him strongly not to go with them, because they would make him become a bad man. Whenever the girls had a play they used to invite Edet Etim, and at last he went to the play, and they made him beat the drum for them to dance to. After much practice he became the best drummer in the town, and whenever the girls had a play they always called him to drum for them. Plenty of the young girls left their husbands, and went to Edet and asked him to marry them. This made all the young men of the town very jealous, and when they met together at night they considered what would be the best way to kill him. At last they decided that when Edet went to bathe they would induce the alligators to take him. So one night, when he was washing, one alligator seized him by the foot, and others came and seized him round the waist. He fought very hard, but at last they dragged him into the deep water, and took him to their home.

When his mother heard this, she determined to do her best to recover her son, so she kept quite quiet until the morning.

When the young men saw that Edet's mother remained quiet, and did not cry, they thought of the story of the hawk and the owl, and determined to keep Edet alive for a few months.

At cockcrow the mother raised a cry, and went to the grave of her dead husband in order to consult his spirit as to what she had better do to recover her lost son. After a time she went down to the beach with small young green branches in her hands, with which she beat the water, and called upon all the Ju Jus of the Calabar River to help her to recover her son. She then went home and got a load of rods, and took them to a Ju Ju man in the farm. His name was Ininen Okon; he was so called because he was very artful, and had plenty of strong Ju Jus.

When the young boys heard that Edet's mother had gone to Ininen Okon, they all trembled with fear, and wanted to return Edet, but they could not do so, as it was against the rules of their society. The Ju Ju man having discovered that Edet was still alive, and was being detained in the alligators' house, told the mother to be patient. After three days Ininen himself joined another alligators' society, and went to inspect the young alligators' house. He found a young man whom he knew, left on guard when all the alligators had gone to feed at the ebb of the tide, and came back and told the mother to wait, as he would make a Ju Ju which would cause them all to depart in seven days, and leave no one in the house. He made his Ju Ju, and the young alligators said that, as no one had come for Edet, they would all go at the ebb tide to feed, and leave no one in charge of the house. When they returned they found Edet still there, and everything as they had left it, as Ininen had not gone that day.

Three days afterwards they all went away again, and this time went a long way off, and did not return quickly. When Ininen saw that the tide was going down he changed himself into an alligator, and swam to the young alligators' home, where he found Edet chained to a post. He then found an axe and cut the post, releasing the boy. But Edet, having been in the water so long, was deaf and dumb. He then found several loin cloths which had been left behind by the young alligators, so he gathered them together and took them away to show to the king, and Ininen left the place, taking Edet with him.

He then called the mother to see her son, but when she came the boy could only look at her, and could not speak. The mother embraced her boy, but he took no notice, as he did not seem capable of understanding anything, but sat down quietly. Then the Ju Ju man told Edet's mother that he would cure her son in a few days, so he made several Ju Jus, and gave her son medicine, and after a time the boy recovered his speech and became sensible again.

Then Edet's mother put on a mourning cloth, and pretended that her son was dead, and did not tell the people he had come back to her. When the young alligators returned, they found that Edet was gone, and that some one had taken their loin cloths. They were therefore much afraid, and made inquiries if Edet had been seen, but they could hear nothing about him, as he was hidden in a farm, and the mother continued to wear her mourning cloth in order to deceive them.

Nothing happened for six months, and they had quite forgotten all about the matter. Affiong, the mother, then went to the chiefs of the town, and asked them to hold a large meeting of all the people, both young and old, at the palaver house, so that her late husband's property might be divided up in accordance with the native custom, as her son had been killed by the alligators.

The next day the chiefs called all the people together, but the mother in the early morning took her son to a small room at the back of the palaver house, and left him there with the seven loin cloths which the Ju Ju man had taken from the alligators' home. When the chiefs and all the people were seated, Affiong stood up and addressed them, saying—

"Chiefs and young men of my town, eight years ago my husband was a fine young man. He married me, and we lived together for many years without having any children. At last I had a son, but my husband died a few months afterwards. I brought my boy up carefully, but as he was a good drummer and dancer the young men were jealous, and had him caught by the alligators. Is there any one present who can tell me what my son would have become if he had lived?" She then asked them what they thought of the alligator society, which had killed so many young men.

The chiefs, who had lost a lot of slaves, told her that if she could produce evidence against any members of the society they would destroy it at once. She then called upon Ininen to appear with her son Edet. He came out from the room leading Edet by the hand, and placed the bundle of loin cloths before the chiefs.

The young men were very much surprised when they saw Edet, and wanted to leave the palaver house; but when they stood up to go the chiefs told them to sit down at once, or they would receive three hundred lashes. They then sat down, and the Ju Ju man explained how he had gone to the alligators' home, and had brought Edet back to his mother. He also said that he had found the seven loin cloths in the house, but he did not wish to say anything about them, as the owners of some of the cloths were sons of the chiefs.

The chiefs, who were anxious to stop the bad society, told him, however, to speak at once and tell them everything. Then he undid the bundle and took the cloths out one by one, at the same time calling upon the owners to come and take them. When they came to take their cloths, they were told to remain where they were; and they were then told to name their company. The seven young men then gave the names of all the members of their society, thirty-two in all. These men were all placed in a line, and the chiefs then passed sentence, which was that they should all be killed the next morning on the beach. So they were then all tied together to posts, and seven men were placed as a guard over them. They made fires and beat drums all the night.

Early in the morning, at about 4 a.m., the big wooden drum was placed on the roof of the palaver house, and beaten to celebrate the death of the evildoers, which was the custom in those days.

The boys were then unfastened from the posts, and had their hands tied behind their backs, and were marched down to the beach. When they arrived there, the head chief stood up and addressed the people. "This is a small town of which I am chief, and I am determined to stop this bad custom, as so many men have been killed." He then told a man who had a sharp matchet to cut off one man's head. He then told another man who had a sharp knife to skin another young man alive. A third man who had a heavy stick was ordered to beat another to death, and so the chief went on and killed all the thirty-two young men in the most horrible ways he could think of. Some of them were tied to posts in the river, and left there until the tide came up and drowned them. Others were flogged to death.

After they had all been killed, for many years no one was killed by alligators, but some little time afterwards on the road between the beach and the town the land fell in, making a very large and deep hole, which was said to be the home of the alligators, and the people have ever since tried to fill it up, but have never yet been able to do so.

Mkaaah Jeechonee, the Boy Hunter

Sultan Maaj'noon had seven sons and a big cat, of all of whom he was very proud.

Everything went well until one day the cat went and caught a calf. When they told the sultan he said, "Well, the cat is mine, and the calf is mine." So they said, "Oh, all right, master," and let the matter drop.

A few days later the cat caught a goat; and when they told the sultan he said, "The cat is mine, and the goat is mine;" and so that settled it again.

Two days more passed, and the cat caught a cow. They told the sultan, and he shut them up with "My cat, and my cow."

After another two days the cat caught a donkey; same result.

Next it caught a horse; same result.

The next victim was a camel; and when they told the sultan he said: "What's the matter with you folks? It was my cat, and my camel. I believe you don't like my cat, and want it killed, bringing me tales about it every day. Let it eat whatever it wants to."

In a very short time it caught a child, and then a full-grown man; but each time the sultan remarked that both the cat and its victim were his, and thought no more of it.

Meantime the cat grew bolder, and hung around a low, open place near the town, pouncing on people going for water, or animals out at pasture, and eating them.

At last some of the people plucked up courage; and, going to the sultan, said: "How is this, master? As you are our sultan you are our protector,—or ought to be,—yet you have allowed this cat to do as it pleases, and now it lives just out of town there, and kills everything living that goes that way, while at night it comes into town and does the same thing. Now, what on earth are we to do?"

But Maajnoon only replied: "I really believe you hate my cat. I suppose you want me to kill it; but I shall do no such thing. Everything it eats is mine."

Of course the folks were astonished at this result of the interview, and, as no one dared to kill the cat, they all had to remove from the vicinity where it lived. But this did not mend matters, because, when it found no one came that way, it shifted its quarters likewise.

So complaints continued to pour in, until at last Sultan Maajnoon gave orders that if any one came to make accusations against the cat, he was to be informed that the master could not be seen.

When things got so that people neither let their animals out nor went out themselves, the cat went farther into the country, killing and eating cattle, and fowls, and everything that came its way.

One day the sultan said to six of his sons, "I'm going to look at the country to-day; come along with me."

The seventh son was considered too young to go around anywhere, and was always left at home with the women folk, being called by his brothers Mkaa'ah Jeecho'nee, which means Mr. Sit-in-the-kitchen.

Well, they went, and presently came to a thicket. The father was in front and the six sons following him, when the cat jumped out and killed three of the latter.

The attendants shouted, "The cat! the cat!" and the soldiers asked permission to search for and kill it, which the sultan readily granted, saying: "This is not a cat, it is a noon'dah. It has taken from me my own sons."

Now, nobody had ever seen a noondah, but they all knew it was a terrible beast that could kill and eat all other living things.

When the sultan began to bemoan the loss of his sons, some of those who heard him said: "Ah, master, this noondah does not select his prey. He doesn't say: 'This is my master's son, I'll leave him alone,' or, 'This is my master's wife, I won't eat her.' When we told you what the cat had done, you always said it was your cat, and what it ate was yours, and now it has killed your sons, and we don't believe it would hesitate to eat even you."

And he said, "I fear you are right."

As for the soldiers who tried to get the cat, some were killed and the remainder ran away, and the sultan and his living sons took the dead bodies home and buried them.

Now when Mkaaah Jeechonee, the seventh son, heard that his brothers had been killed by the noondah, he said to his mother, "I, too, will go, that it may kill me as well as my brothers, or I will kill it."

But his mother said: "My son, I do not like to have you go. Those three are already dead; and if you are killed also, will not that be one wound upon another to my heart?"

"Nevertheless," said he, "I can not help going; but do not tell my father."

So his mother made him some cakes, and sent some attendants with him; and he took a great spear, as sharp as a razor, and a sword, bade her farewell, and departed.

As he had always been left at home, he had no very clear idea what he was going to hunt for; so he had not gone far beyond the suburbs, when, seeing a very large dog, he concluded that this was the animal he was after; so he killed it, tied a rope to it, and dragged it home, singing,

"Oh, mother, I have killed

The noondah, eater of the people."

When his mother, who was upstairs, heard him, she looked out of the window, and, seeing what he had brought, said, "My son, this is not the noondah, eater of the people."

So he left the carcass outside and went in to talk about it, and his mother said, "My dear boy, the noondah is a much larger animal than that; but if I were you, I'd give the business up and stay at home."

"No, indeed," he exclaimed; "no staying at home for me until I have met and fought the noondah."

So he set out again, and went a great deal farther than he had gone on the former day. Presently he saw a civet cat, and, believing it to be the animal he was in search of, he killed it, bound it, and dragged it home, singing,

"Oh, mother, I have killed

The noondah, eater of the people."

When his mother saw the civet cat, she said, "My son, this is not the noondah, eater of the people." And he threw it away.

Again his mother entreated him to stay at home, but he would not listen to her, and started off again.

This time he went away off into the forest, and seeing a bigger cat than the last one, he killed it, bound it, and dragged it home, singing,

"Oh, mother, I have killed

The noondah, eater of the people."

But directly his mother saw it, she had to tell him, as before, "My son, this is not the noondah, eater of the people."

He was, of course, very much troubled at this; and his mother said, "Now, where do you expect to find this noondah? You don't know where it is, and you don't know what it looks like. You'll get sick over this; you're not looking so well now as you did. Come, stay at home."

But he said: "There are three things, one of which I shall do: I shall die; I shall find the noondah and kill it; or I shall return home unsuccessful. In any case, I'm off again."

This time he went farther than before, saw a zebra, killed it, bound it, and dragged it home, singing,

"Oh, mother, I have killed

The noondah, eater of the people."

Of course his mother had to tell him, once again, "My son, this is not the noondah, eater of the people."

After a good deal of argument, in which his mother's persuasion, as usual, was of no avail, he went off again, going farther than ever, when he caught a giraffe; and when he had killed it he said: "Well, this time I've been successful. This must be the noondah." So he dragged it home, singing,

"Oh, mother, I have killed

The noondah, eater of the people."

Again his mother had to assure him, "My son, this is not the noondah, eater of the people." She then pointed out to him that his brothers were not running about hunting for the noondah, but staying at home attending to their own business. But, remarking that all brothers were not alike, he expressed his determination to stick to his task until it came to a successful termination, and went off again, a still greater distance than before.

While going through the wilderness he espied a rhinoceros asleep under a tree, and turning to his attendants he exclaimed, "At last I see the noondah."

"Where, master?" they all cried, eagerly.

"There, under the tree."

"Oh-h! What shall we do?" they asked.

And he answered: "First of all, let us eat our fill, then we will attack it.
We have found it in a good place, though if it kills us, we can't help it."

So they all took out their arrowroot cakes and ate till they were satisfied.

Then Mkaaah Jeechonee said, "Each of you take two guns; lay one beside you and take the other in your hands, and at the proper time let us all fire at once."

And they said, "All right, master."

So they crept cautiously through the bushes and got around to the other side of the tree, at the back of the rhinoceros; then they closed up till they were quite near it, and all fired together. The beast jumped up, ran a little way, and then fell down dead.

They bound it, and dragged it for two whole days, until they reached the town, when Mkaaah Jeechonee began singing,

"Oh, mother, I have killed

The noondah, eater of the people."

But he received the same answer from his mother: "My

son, this is not the noondah, eater of the people."

And many persons came and looked at the rhinoceros, and felt very sorry for the young man. As for his father and mother, they both begged of him to give up, his father offering to give him anything he possessed if he would only stay at home. But he said, "I don't hear what you are saying; good-bye," and was off again.

This time he still further increased the distance from his home, and at last he saw an elephant asleep at noon in the forest. Thereupon he said to his attendants, "Now we have found the noondah."

"Ah, where is he?" said they.

"Yonder, in the shade. Do you see it?"

"Oh, yes, master; shall we march up to it?"

"If we march up to it, and it is looking this way, it will come at us, and if it does that, some of us will be killed. I think we had best let one man steal up close and see which way its face is turned."

As every one thought this was a good idea, a slave named Keerobo'to crept on his hands and knees, and had a good look at it. When he returned in the same manner, his master asked: "Well, what's the news? Is it the noondah?"

"I do not know," replied Keeroboto; "but I think there is very little doubt that it is. It is broad, with a very big head, and, goodness, I never saw such large ears!"

"All right," said Mkaaah Jeechonee; "let us eat, and then go for it."

So they took their arrowroot cakes, and their molasses cakes, and ate until they were quite full.

Then the youth said to them: "My people, to-day is perhaps the last we shall ever see; so we will take leave of each other. Those who are to escape will escape, and those who are to die will die; but if I die, let those who escape tell my mother and father not to grieve for me."

But his attendants said, "Oh, come along, master; none of us will die, please God."

So they went on their hands and knees till they were close up, and then they said to Mkaaah Jeechonee, "Give us your plan, master;" but he said, "There is no plan, only let all fire at once."

Well, they fired all at once, and immediately the elephant jumped up and charged at them. Then such a helter-skelter flight as there was! They threw away their guns and everything they carried, and made for the trees, which they climbed with surprising alacrity.

As to the elephant, he kept straight ahead until he fell down some distance away.

They all remained in the trees from three until six o'clock in the morning, without food and without clothing.

The young man sat in his tree and wept bitterly, saying, "I don't exactly know what death is, but it seems to me this must be very like it." As no one could see any one else, he did not know where his attendants were, and though he wished to come down from the tree, he thought, "Maybe the noondah is down below there, and will eat me."

Each attendant was in exactly the same fix, wishing to come down, but afraid the noondah was waiting to eat him.

Keeroboto had seen the elephant fall, but was afraid to get down by himself, saying, "Perhaps, though it has fallen down, it is not dead." But presently he saw a dog go up to it and smell it, and then he was sure it was dead. Then he got down from the tree as fast as he could and gave a signal cry, which was answered; but not being sure from whence the answer came, he repeated the cry, listening intently. When it was answered he went straight to the place from which the sound proceeded, and found two of his companions in one tree. To them he said, "Come on; get down; the noondah is dead." So they got down quickly and hunted around until they found their master. When they told him the news, he came down also; and after a little the attendants had all gathered together and had picked up their guns and their clothes, and were all right again. But they were all weak and hungry, so they rested and ate some food, after which they went to examine their prize.

As soon as Mkaaah Jeechonee saw it he said, "Ah, this is the noondah!
This is it! This is it!" And they all agreed that it was it.

So they dragged the elephant three days to their town, and then the youth began singing,
"Oh, mother, this is he,

The noondah, eater of the people."

He was, naturally, quite upset when his mother replied, "My son, this is not the noondah, eater of the people." She further said: "Poor boy! what trouble you have been through. All the people are astonished that one so young should have such a great understanding!"

Then his father and mother began their entreaties again, and finally it was agreed that this next trip should be his last, whatever the result might be.

Well, they started off again, and went on and on, past the forest, until they came to a very high mountain, at the foot of which they camped for the night.

In the morning they cooked their rice and ate it, and then Mkaaah Jeechonee said: "Let us now climb the mountain, and look all over the country from its peak." And they went and they went, until after a long, weary while, they reached the top, where they sat down to rest and form their plans.

Now, one of the attendants, named Shindaa'no, while walking about, cast his eyes down the side of the mountain, and suddenly saw a great beast about half way down; but he could not make out its appearance distinctly, on account of the distance and the trees. Calling his master, he pointed it out to him, and something in Mkaaah Jeechonee's heart told him that it was the noondah. To make sure, however, he took his gun and his spear and went partly down the mountain to get a better view.

"Ah," said he, "this must be the noondah. My mother told me its ears were small, and those are small; she told me the noondah is broad and short, and so is this; she said it has two blotches, like a civet cat, and there are the blotches; she told me the tail is thick, and there is a thick tail. It must be the noondah."

Then he went back to his attendants and bade them eat heartily, which they did. Next he told them to leave every unnecessary thing behind, because if they had to run they would be better without encumbrance, and if they were victorious they could return for their goods.

When they had made all their arrangements they started down the mountain, but when they had got about half way down Keeroboto and Shindaano were afraid. Then the youth said to them: "Oh, let's go on; don't be afraid. We all have to live and die. What are you frightened about?" So, thus encouraged, they went on.

When they came near the place, Mkaaah Jeechonee ordered them to take off all their clothing except one piece, and to place that tightly on their bodies, so that if they had to run they would not be caught by thorns or branches.

So when they came close to the beast, they saw that it was asleep, and all agreed that it was the noondah.

Then the young man said, "Now the sun is setting, shall we fire at it, or let be till morning?"

And they all wished to fire at once, and see what the result would be without further tax on their nerves; therefore they arranged that they should all fire together.

They all crept up close, and when the master gave the word, they discharged their guns together. The noondah did not move; that one dose had been sufficient. Nevertheless, they all turned and scampered up to the top of the mountain. There they ate and rested for the night.

In the morning they ate their rice, and then went down to see how matters were, when they found the beast lying dead.

After resting and eating, they started homeward, dragging the dead beast with them. On the fourth day it began to give indications of decay, and the attendants wished to abandon it; but Mkaaah Jeechonee said they would continue to drag it if there was only one bone left.

When they came near the town he began to sing,

"Mother, mother, I have come

From the evil spirits, home.

Mother, listen while I sing;

While I tell you what I bring.

Oh, mother, I have killed

The noondah, eater of the people."

And when his mother looked out, she cried, "My son, this is the noondah, eater of the people."

Then all the people came out to welcome him, and his father was overcome with joy, and loaded him with honors, and procured him a rich and beautiful wife; and when he died Mkaaah Jeechonee became sultan, and lived long and happily, beloved by all the people.

Pretty Girl and the Seven Jealous Women

There was once a very beautiful girl called Akim. She was a native of Ibibio, and the name was given to her on account of her good looks, as she was born in the spring-time. She was an only daughter, and her parents were extremely fond of her. The people of the town, and more particularly the young girls, were so jealous of Akim's good looks and beautiful form—for she was perfectly made, very strong, and her carriage, bearing, and manners were most graceful—that her parents would not allow her to join the young girls' society in the town, as is customary for all young people to do, both boys and girls belonging to a company according to their age; a company consisting, as a rule, of all the boys or girls born in the same year.

Akim's parents were rather poor, but she was a good

daughter, and gave them no trouble, so they had a happy home. One day as Akim was on her way to draw water from the spring she met the company of seven girls, to which in an ordinary way she would have belonged, if her parents had not forbidden her. These girls told her that they were going to hold a play in the town in three days' time, and asked her to join them. She said she was very sorry, but that her parents were poor, and only had herself to work for them, she therefore had no time to spare for dancing and plays. She then left them and went home.

In the evening the seven girls met together, and as they were very envious of Akim, they discussed how they should be revenged upon her for refusing to join their company, and they talked for a long time as to how they could get Akim into danger or punish her in some way.

At last one of the girls suggested that they should all go to Akim's house every day and help her with her work, so that when they had made friends with her they would be able to entice her away and take their revenge upon her for being more beautiful than themselves. Although they went every day and helped Akim and her parents with their work, the parents knew that they were jealous of their daughter, and repeatedly warned her not on any account to go with them, as they were not to be trusted.

At the end of the year there was going to be a big play, called the new yam play, to which Akim's parents had been invited. The play was going to be held at a town about two hours' march from where they lived. Akim was very anxious to go and take part in the dance, but her parents gave her plenty of work to do before they started, thinking that this would surely prevent her going, as she was a very obedient daughter, and always did her work properly.

On the morning of the play the jealous seven came to Akim and asked her to go with them, but she pointed to all the water-pots she had to fill, and showed them where her parents had told her to polish the walls with a stone and make the floor good; and after that was finished she had to pull up all the weeds round the house and clean up all round. She therefore said it was impossible for her to leave the house until all the work was finished. When the girls heard this they took up the water-pots, went to the spring, and quickly returned with them full; they placed them in a row, and then they got stones, and very soon had the walls polished and the floor made good; after that they did the weeding outside and the cleaning up, and when everything was completed they said to Akim, "Now then, come along; you have no excuse to remain behind, as all the work is done."

Akim really wanted to go to the play; so as all the work was done which her parents had told her to do, she finally consented to go. About half-way to the town, where the new yam play was being held, there was a small river, about five feet deep, which had to be crossed by wading, as there was no bridge. In this river there was a powerful Ju Ju, whose law was that whenever any one crossed the river and returned the same way on the return journey, whoever it was, had to give some food to the Ju Ju. If they did not make the proper sacrifice the Ju Ju dragged them down and took them to his home, and kept them there to work for him. The seven jealous girls knew all about this Ju Ju, having often crossed the river before, as they walked about all over the country, and had plenty of friends in the different towns. Akim, however, who was a good girl, and never went anywhere, knew nothing about

this Ju Ju, which her
companions had found out.

When the work was finished
they all started off together,
and crossed the river without
any trouble. When they had
gone a small distance on the
other side they saw a small
bird, perched on a high tree,
who admired Akim very much,
and sang in praise of her
beauty, much to the annoyance
of the seven girls; but they
walked on without saying
anything, and eventually
arrived at the town where the
play was being held. Akim had
not taken the trouble to change

her clothes, but when she arrived at the town, although her companions had on all their best beads and their finest clothes, the young men and people admired Akim far more than the other girls, and she was declared to be the finest and most beautiful woman at the dance. They gave her plenty of palm wine, foo-foo, and everything she wanted, so that the seven girls became more angry and jealous than before. The people danced and sang all that night, but Akim managed to keep out of the sight of her parents until the following morning, when they asked her how it was that she had disobeyed them and neglected her work; so Akim told them that the work had all been done by her friends, and they had enticed her to come to the play with them. Her mother then told her to return home at once, and that she was not to remain in the town any longer.

When Akim told her friends this they said, "Very well, we are just going to have some small meal, and then we will return with you." They all then sat down together and had their food, but each of the seven jealous girls hid a small quantity of foo-foo and fish in her clothes for the Water Ju Ju. However Akim, who knew nothing about this, as her parents had forgotten to tell her about the Ju Ju, never thinking for one moment that their daughter would cross the river, did not take any food as a sacrifice to the Ju Ju with her.

When they arrived at the river Akim saw the girls making their small sacrifices, and begged them to give her a small share so that she could do the same, but they refused, and all walked across the river safely.

Then when it was Akim's turn to cross, when she arrived in the middle of the river, the Water Ju Ju caught hold of her and dragged her underneath the water, so that she immediately disappeared from sight. The seven girls had been watching for this, and when they saw that she had gone they went on their way, very pleased at the success of their scheme, and said to one another, "Now Akim is gone for ever, and we shall hear no more about her being better-looking than we are."

As there was no one to be seen at the time when Akim disappeared they naturally thought that their cruel action had escaped detection, so they went home rejoicing; but they never noticed the little bird high up in the tree who had sung of Akim's beauty when they were on their way to the play. The little bird was very sorry for Akim, and made up his mind that, when the proper time came, he would tell her parents what he had seen, so that perhaps they would be able to save her. The bird had heard Akim asking for a small portion of the food to make a sacrifice with, and had heard all the girls refusing to give her any.

The following morning, when Akim's parents returned home, they were much surprised to find that the door was fastened, and that there was no sign of their daughter anywhere about the place, so they inquired of their neighbours, but no one was able to give them any information about her. They then went to the seven girls, and asked them what had become of Akim. They replied that they did not know what had become of her, but that she had reached their town safely with them, and then said she was going home. The father then went to his Ju Ju man, who, by casting lots, discovered what had happened, and told him that on her way back from the play Akim had crossed the river without making the customary sacrifice to the Water Ju Ju, and that, as the Ju Ju was angry, he had seized Akim and taken her to his home. He therefore told Akim's father to take one goat, one basketful of eggs, and one piece of white cloth to the river in the morning, and to offer them as a sacrifice to the Water Ju Ju;

then Akim would be thrown out of the water seven times, but that if her father failed to catch her on the seventh time, she would disappear for ever.

Akim's father then returned home, and, when he arrived there, the little bird who had seen Akim taken by the Water Ju Ju, told him everything that had happened, confirming the Ju Ju's words. He also said that it was entirely the fault of the seven girls, who had refused to give Akim any food to make the sacrifice with.

Early the following morning the parents went to the river, and made the sacrifice as advised by the Ju Ju. Immediately they had done so, the Water Ju Ju threw Akim up from the middle of the river. Her father caught her at once, and returned home very thankfully.

He never told any one, however, that he had recovered his daughter, but made up his mind to punish the seven jealous girls, so he dug a deep pit in the middle of his house, and placed dried palm leaves and sharp stakes in the bottom of the pit. He then covered the top of the pit with new mats, and sent out word for all people to come and hold a play to rejoice with him, as he had recovered his daughter from the spirit land. Many people came, and danced and sang all the day and night, but the seven jealous girls did not appear, as they were frightened. However, as they were told that everything had gone well on the previous day, and that there had been no trouble, they went to the house the following morning and mixed with the dancers; but they were ashamed to look Akim in the face, who was sitting down in the middle of the dancing ring.

When Akim's father saw the seven girls he pretended to welcome them as his daughter's friends, and presented each of them with a brass rod, which he placed round their necks. He also gave them tombo to drink.

He then picked them out, and told them to go and sit on mats on the other side of the pit he had prepared for them. When they walked over the mats which hid the pit they all fell in, and Akim's father immediately got some red-hot ashes from the fire and threw them in on top of the screaming girls, who were in great pain. At once the dried palm leaves caught fire, killing all the girls at once.

When the people heard the cries and saw the smoke, they all ran back to the town.

The next day the parents of the dead girls went to the head chief, and complained that Akim's father had killed their daughters, so the chief called him before him, and asked him for an explanation.

Akim's father went at once to the chief, taking the Ju Ju man, whom everybody relied upon, and the small bird, as his witnesses.

When the chief had heard the whole case, he told Akim's father that he should only have killed one girl to avenge his daughter, and not seven. So he told the father to bring Akim before him.

When she arrived, the head chief, seeing how beautiful she was, said that her father was justified in killing all the seven girls on her behalf, so he

dismissed the case, and told
the parents of the dead girls to
go away and mourn for their
daughters, who had been
wicked and jealous women,
and had been properly
punished for their cruel
behaviour to Akim.

Printed in Great Britain
by Amazon

11384760R00130